# THE WEE CHRISTMAS CABIN

retold by Margaret Hodges

illustrated by Kimberly Bulcken Root

Holiday House / New York

*I will arise and go now, and go to Innisfree,*
*And a small cabin build there. . . .*
Wɪʟʟɪᴀᴍ Bᴜᴛʟᴇʀ Yᴇᴀᴛs

Text copyright © 2009 by Margaret Hodges
Retold from "The Wee Christmas Cabin of Carn-na-Ween"
in *The Long Christmas* by Ruth Sawyer. New York: Viking, 1941.
Illustrations copyright © 2009 by Kimberly Bulcken Root
All Rights Reserved
HOLIDAY HOUSE is registered in the U.S. Patent and Trademark Office.
Printed in the United States of America
The illustrations in this book were created
with Winsor & Newton watercolors on 140-lb hot press watercolor paper.
The typeface is Hightower.
www.holidayhouse.com
First Edition
1 3 5 7 9 10 8 6 4 2

Library of Congress Cataloging-in-Publication Data
Hodges, Margaret, 1911-2005.
The wee Christmas cabin / retold by Margaret Hodges ;
illustrated by Kimberly Bulcken Root. — 1st ed.
p. cm.
"Retold from the 'Wee Christmas cabin of Carn-na-ween'
in the Long Christmas by Ruth Sawyer ... 1941"—
Summary: A tinker's child who grows up helping everyone in her Irish village
is rewarded in her old age with a cabin built by fairies on Christmas Eve.
ISBN-10: 0-8234-1528-7 (hardcover)
ISBN-13: 978-0-8234-1528-1
[1. Fairies—Fiction. 2. Ireland—Fiction. 3. Christmas—Fiction.]
I. Root, Kimberly Bulcken, ill. II. Title.
PZ7.H6644We 2001
[E]—dc21
00-044877

To Ruth Sawyer
M. H.

For my friend Janet Sheehan
and her talented family,
and for Coach Dolan's
daughters
K. B. R.

Long ago, an Irish village straggled along a road that led to the sea. Between the village and the sea, fairies lived under a thornbush, and one night they saw a drove of tinkers leaving a newborn baby girl upon the doorsill of a cabin.

The cabin belonged to Bridget and Conal Hegarty. Bridget nursed the wee thing with her own baby and loved her as her own. She named her Oona, and Oona grew into the prettiest and gentlest-mannered lass in the county.

Bridget did her best to get the lads to court her, but the lads would have none of her. Their feet might be itching to take her to a crossroads dance. But marry a tinker's child? No! And so Oona never had a chance to marry and have children of her own, or a cabin she could call hers.

When all of Bridget and Conal's children had married, Oona stayed on to mind the house for Bridget and Conal, and to care for them through their sicknesses. From the beginning she had a dream that the Hegartys would at long last be leaving her their cabin for her own. But Bridget, before she died, broke the dream.

"Our cabin goes to our son Michael, and he won't need you," she said. "But take your share of the linen. Some man, losing his wife, may be glad to take you for his second. I'd not have you going to him empty-handed." Oona moved on.

From cabin to cabin, wherever there was trouble or need there was Oona. Where a young mother was ailing, you would find Oona caring for the child as if it were her own. In a cabin where a man had lost his wife and was ill fitted to mind the house and the wee ones alone, here she was the happiest.

Those she served saw that she never went away empty-handed. So to Bridget Hegarty's linen was added a griddle, pans, kettles, and dishes. As the years went by, the bundle of Oona's possessions grew.

She was not downhearted. "You never can tell," she would say. "I may yet have a wee cabin of my own someday. I'm not saying how, and I'm not saying when."

She was in the cabin of the MacManuses when the great famine came. The corn in the fields was blighted. The potatoes rotted in the ground. There was neither food for man nor fodder for beasts.

Oona had grown so old that she moved slowly on unsteady feet. But she milked, she churned, she helped cut the turf to keep a fire burning on the hearth. So long as there was food enough, the MacManuses kept her and were thankful for another pair of hands to work. But as the winter drew in, Oona saw the children watching every morsel of food she put to her lips.

A night came when the spoon scraped the bottom of the meal-bin and the last of the potatoes had been eaten, skins and all. Saying never a word, Oona started to put her things into her bundle. As she lifted the latch, she spoke. "You can take care of yourselves. You won't need me now."

"Aye, 'tis God's truth," said the wife.

"Hush, remember what night it is," said Timothy MacManus.

"'Tis Christmas Eve. What matter? In times such as these, one night is like another."

"God and Mary stay with you this night," Oona called, going out the door.

"God and Mary go with you," the two mumbled back at her.

Outside, Oona took the road leading to the sea. A light snow was falling. As she went along the village street, she looked into the lighted windows of each cabin. Hardly a cabin but she had lived in. Her lips made a blessing and a farewell for every door she passed.

When all the cabins were left behind, she stumbled at last from the road to find shelter under a blackthorn bush.

"I like it here," she said as she eased her bundle from her back. "Many's the time I have said, 'Sometime I will take the whole day and sit under this very thornbush, to feel the wind from the sea and watch the sun and the stars and maybe hear the sound of fairy pipes.' I never had a whole day."

After that, her head grew light. She lost all count of time. She felt no cold, no tiredness. She slept a little, woke, and slept again. Snow had covered her, warm.

Tomorrow would be a white Christmas, and people had a saying that on a white Christmas the fairies trooped out to see the wonder of it. Aye, that was a good saying.

Oona tried to move her legs, and as she did she had a strange feeling that she had knocked something over. Her hand groped for whatever it was that she had upset. To her amazement, when she held her hand under her eyes, there was a fairy man, not a hand high. His wee face was puckered with worry.

"Don't be afraid, wee man," she clucked to him. "Was there anything at all you were wanting?"

"Aye, we were wanting you."

"Me?"

"None else. Look!"

And then she saw the ground about her covered with hundreds upon hundreds of fairies, their faces no bigger than buttons, all laughing.

"What might you be laughing at?" she asked.

"We're laughing at you, tinker's child. Living a lifetime in other folks' cabins, serving and nursing and mothering and loving, and never a cabin you could call your own. Stay where you are, Oona Hegarty, and sleep."

She did as she was bidden, but sleep was as thin as the snow that covered her, so that she could see through it what was going on about her. Hither and yon the fairies were hurrying. They brought stones; they brought turf. They laid a thatched roof. They built a chimney and put in windows. They hung a door at the front and a door at the back. Then she felt a small, tweaking hand on her skirt and heard a shrill voice piping, "Wake up—wake up, Oona Hegarty!"

"I am awake," said Oona, sitting up and rubbing her eyes. "Awake and dreaming at the same time."

"We'll be fetching in your bundle, then," said the voice, "and all things shall find their rightful places at last."

Ten hundred fairy men lifted the bundle and bore it inside the little house, with Oona following. She drew her breath and let it out again.

"Is everything to your liking, ma'am?" inquired the fairy she had knocked over. Oona looked about her. "The bed's where it should be. The dresser is convenient. Wait till I have my bundle undone."

The fairies scuttled about helping her, putting the linen in the fine oak chest, the dishes on the shelves. The kettle was hung above the hearth, the stool set beside it. All things in their right places as the tinker's child had dreamed them.

"Is it all to your liking?" shouted the fairies together.

"Aye, it's that and more. I only ask one thing. On every white Christmas, bring folk to my door, old ones not needed any longer by others, children crying for their mothers, lads or lasses in trouble. Fetch them so that I may warm them by the hearth and comfort them."

"We will do that, tinker's child!" The voices of the fairies drifted away. Oona drew the curtains, lay down in the bed, and pulled the warm blanket over herself.

The next night—Christmas—hunger drove Maggie,
the MacManuses' middle child, out of their cabin, blindly
stumbling along the road. Then, rubbing her eyes, she
looked up at the wee cabin standing where no cabin had
ever been. Through the windows came a welcoming light.
In wonderment she lifted the latch and went in.

"I have been looking for you, Maggie." It was Oona's voice, but what a change! Oona herself, grown young, with the look of a young bride. She sat by the fire, turning the griddle bread. There were potatoes boiling in the kettle and a pot of tea on the hearth. Enough to eat and to spare. Her voice was as low and soft as a bird's calling to its young. "You'll be eating your fill, Maggie, and not be hungry again for many a day."

And it's the truth I'm telling you. Maggie went back and told, but all year long no one could find the cabin. Not until a white Christmas came round again.

So the tales run. This I know. If there is a white Christmas this year, the wee fairy cabin will be having its latch lifted. And Oona Hegarty, the tinker's child, will be keeping the griddle hot, the kettle full, and her arms wide to the children of half the world this night—if it's a white Christmas.